Cool Cat,
School
Cat

Cool Cat, School Cat

BY **Judy Cox**

ILLUSTRATED BY
Blanche Sims

Holiday House/ New York

Library of Congress Cataloging-in-Publication
Cox, Judy.
Cool cat, school cat / by Judy Cox; illustrated by Blanche Sims.—1st ed.
p. cm.
Summary: Eight-year-old, disorganized Gus misses the dog left behind
when his family moved, but then he meets a stray cat and a bossy
classmate who breaks school rules to help him care for it.
ISBN 0-8234-1714-X
[1. Cats—Fiction. 2. Animal rescue—Fiction. 3. Schools—Fiction.
4. Responsibility—Fiction.] I. Sims, Blanche, ill. II. Title.

PZ7.C83835 Co 2002
[Fic]—dc21
2002017103

*With thanks to Tim
who put the story back on track
J. C.*

CONTENTS

Cool Cat,
School
Cat

I. Stray Cat

Gus pounded down the sidewalk. He didn't want to be late on the first day of school.

Gus hoped he was going to like Lake Creek School. But already he missed his old school, and his best friend, Justin. And most of all he missed his dog, Oscar. His old house, his old school, his old friends. Nothing would be the same this year.

He tripped over his shoelace and fell. Darn! He checked for blood. No blood. Good. He bent to tie his shoe.

Something moved underneath the bushes by the sidewalk. What could it be? A bird? A lizard? Gus got down on his hands and knees. Under the bush, eyes glowed like streetlights.

"What are you doing? Didn't you hear the bell? You're going to be late!"

He looked up.

A girl stood over him. A red bow swung on the end of her black ponytail. He'd seen her before. She lived in his building. He didn't know her name. She wore a plaid dress and red shoes. First day of school clothes.

"Something's under there," he said.

The girl bent down. "I don't see anything," she said.

Gus ignored her. There *was* something. He was sure.

The girl carefully set her backpack on the sidewalk and knelt down. "I don't see . . . Yes! There is something!"

Gus leaned closer.

It was a cat. An orange-striped cat with a white bib. He had one blue eye and one green eye. One ear was torn. Some of his whiskers were broken.

"Merow," said the cat. He was a scrawny, scraggly mess.

"Here, kitty," said Gus.

"We'll be late," said the girl. She stood up and dusted off her knees.

"We can't leave this poor kitty," said Gus. "He looks lost."

"It's just a flea-bitten old stray," said the girl. "Leave it alone. My grandmother says never touch animals you don't know. It might bite. Then you'll get rabies."

"If he's a stray, we should help him!"

The girl looked worried. "I can't be late on the first day." She picked up her backpack. "You shouldn't, either."

"Go ahead, then," said Gus. "See if I care. I'm going to rescue this cat."

He didn't look up. But he could tell by the sounds that the girl was leaving. Running, so she wouldn't be late.

Gus rummaged in his backpack for his lunch sack.

Potato chips. Juice. Carrot sticks. No cat food. He unwrapped his sandwich. Yes! Turkey. The cat would love that.

He held out a bit of turkey sandwich. The cat poked his nose out from under the bushes. He sniffed. His eyes narrowed.

Slowly, he crept toward Gus, his belly low to the ground. He snatched the piece of sandwich from Gus. Gus let go, startled. The cat pulled the food toward him. Step by step, he backed up, keeping a wary eye on Gus.

Gus sat back on his heels and watched. The cat stopped under the bushes. He gobbled down the food. Gus lifted his hand to try to pet him.

The cat backed away. "Grrrr," he said.

Gus put his hand back down. He forgot all about school.

This must be a homeless cat. It was so skinny, it must be starving. He'd take it home. It could sleep on his bed. He would name it.

Meanwhile, the cat crept back out of the bushes, sniffing. Gus tore off another piece of sandwich. The cat put out a battered paw and scooped the food toward him.

How am I going to get it home? wondered Gus. Put it in my backpack? No, too small.

He felt in his pockets. Maybe he had something he could use.

His pockets were full. Gus pulled out a lint-covered cough drop. He wiped the cough drop on the grass and popped it in his mouth. Cherry.

The other pocket held an iron key and a green plastic army man. A piece of string lay at the bottom. A leash! He'd lead the cat home.

He pulled the string out of his pocket. It was dingy with dirt. He began untying the knots, talking while he worked.

"Nice kitty," he said. "I'll take care of you." The string was free. Gus tied it in a circle. He'd loop it over the cat's neck to make a collar and leash.

"Come here, nice kitty. Don't be scared." Gus held out the last bite of turkey sandwich. The cat's whiskers twitched. He batted the sandwich, but Gus didn't let go.

The cat crawled out from under the bush. He crept over to Gus, keeping an eye out. He bit the bread.

Gus grabbed him. He pulled the string loop over the cat's head. "Gotcha!" he said. "You're mine, now!"

But the cat didn't want to be leashed. "Sssspppiiitttt!" He hissed. He struggled to get free. His paws raked down Gus's bare arm, leaving deep, raw scratches.

"Ow!" Gus let go. The cat dashed off, the end of the string trailing on the ground behind him.

The scratches bled. Gus wiped them on his shirt, sniffing a little because they hurt. What a way to start the first day.

2. Mr. D

Gus skidded down the hall and through the door of Room 3. He stopped.

A big man stood at the board. His long hair was in a ponytail. A gold earring glittered in one ear. He wore sandals on his feet. He didn't look like any kind of teacher Gus had ever seen before.

"Welcome!" said the man. "Have a seat."

Gus looked around. The class was full. Only one seat was left, next to the same girl he'd seen walking to school. The ponytail girl. He slid into the chair next to hers.

The man wrote something on the board: MR. DHIMITRAKOPOULOUS.

The curvy writing looped across the whole board.

"What's that say?" asked Gus. He didn't want to admit it, but sometimes long words gave him a headache. Like now.

The girl read it out loud, but slowly. "Mister Dhimi-tra-ko-pou-lous," she sounded out.

"Mr. Dhimitrakopoulous. Quite a mouthful, isn't it? But please, call me Mr. D." When Mr. D laughed, his eyes crinkled up at the corners.

"You betcha, Mr. D!" said Gus. Already, he liked this guy.

"Now, I've introduced myself. It's time for me to meet all of you," said Mr. D. "Please raise your hand when I call your name. Brett Chavez."

"Here!" called the boy next to Gus. His dark hair was slicked down, but his brown eyes looked full of fun. Maybe he likes to play army men, thought Gus.

"Pamela Kennedy," said Mr. D.

The girl next to Gus raised her hand.

Mr. D continued down the list. Gus tuned out. He looked around the room. It didn't look like Mrs. Sorem's classroom in his old school. Mrs. Sorem had white rats in a glass tank. Mrs. Sorem had a teddy bear hamster in a cage. Mrs. Sorem had a guinea pig named Lady.

Mr. D only had a couple of parakeets in a wire cage. Parakeets were better than nothing, Gus supposed. But he longed for a mouse or a guinea pig or a rat. Something furry and warm to hold. To pet. A pet you could pet. Yeah.

Gus became aware of silence.

"Gus Zander," repeated Mr. D.

Gus looked up. Everyone looked at him.

It was his chance to make an impression. Quickly, he stuck two pencils under his upper lip. They dangled like fangs.

"I am Count Dracula! I vant to suck your blood!" He lunged at Pamela. That gag always made Justin laugh.

But Pamela didn't. She pulled away and looked disgusted. "Mr. D!" she said. "Can I move?"

"Sorry, Pamela," said Mr. D. "As you can see, our class is full. Gus, have a little respect for your seat mates." He sounded stern, but Gus saw him smile.

Gus pulled the pencils out of his mouth. "Okay, Mr. D. Whatever you say." When Mr. D turned around, Gus put his thumbs in his ears and waved at Pamela. She made a face.

"I have a little surprise for you," Mr. D said. "A week from Saturday, the whole class gets to go on a field trip. We'll go swimming at the city pool, and then have pizza at Pizza Pit Stop."

Everyone cheered. If every day is like this, I'm going to love this school, thought Gus.

The red-bow girl raised her hand. "Yes, Pamela?" asked Mr. D.

"My dad is coming a week from Saturday. I can't go."

"I'm sorry," said Mr. D. "But we'll plan other excursions. You'll be able to go another time."

Pamela nodded, but Gus thought she looked sad. Tough luck.

"I'll hand out the permission slips now," said Mr. D. "Be sure to get them signed and bring them back by next Friday. Remember, you can't go if you don't have a signed permission slip."

Gus grabbed his slip and dropped it. He stepped on it, leaving a black footprint. The corner tore when he tried to pick it up. Well, that wouldn't matter. He crammed it inside his backpack.

Pamela carefully unzipped her backpack. She took out her binder and slid the permission slip inside. Gus wondered why she bothered since she couldn't go.

"Pamela Kennedy," read a tag on her backpack. Pamela Canal, thought Gus. She saw him looking at her and frowned. He knew the kind of girl. Smart. Organized. Bossy. Not somebody he'd want to be friends with. No sir.

3. No Pets Allowed

Rain peppered the sidewalk when Gus left school. He'd forgotten his coat, but he didn't mind. The rain cooled his skin. Autumn would be here soon. Already the leaves were changing.

Gus stomped in a puddle. Drops of water shot up and cascaded back on his feet. Something wiggled on the wet, gray sidewalk. A worm.

Last year, a man came to talk to Mrs. Sorem's class. "Worms are our friends," the man told the class. "They help the soil." Gus remembered they can drown in puddles, too. And if you see a worm, you shouldn't squish it.

Gus bent to look at this worm. It was pink
and gray, with little rings on its soft, squishy-
looking body. It didn't move. Was it dead? Had
it drowned?

He prodded it with his finger. The worm
rolled away from his finger, one little coil after
another. Gus felt a sense of relief. Good, it
hadn't drowned. He picked it up and put it on
the grass. It would be safe there. It could find its
way home to its worm family. Gus pictured the
worm mom: "Goodness gracious! Where have
you been? We've been so worried! You're late
again! You'll have to be grounded!"

He looked at his watch. Gosh! Where had the time gone? He leaped to his feet in a flash, pounding toward home, leaving his backpack on the sidewalk.

Gus dashed up the outside stairs to his apartment.

He lived on the second floor. His old building had an elevator, but Gus didn't mind the stairs. The old manager used to yell at him for riding the elevator. And he'd only ridden it forty-three times! Of course, that was all in a row.

Dad managed this apartment building. Gus was glad Dad finally had a job, after being out of work for six months, but he didn't like the new place at all. He didn't even have his own room, but had to share with Traci.

Worst of all, he couldn't bring Oscar. No pets allowed. Luckily, they'd found a good home for Oscar. And Gus could visit whenever they went back to their old town. But it wasn't the same.

Mom and Traci were in the kitchen. Traci sat in her high chair. Mom fed her cheese cubes.

Traci giggled when she saw Gus. Gus kissed the top of her head. She was too sticky to kiss anywhere else.

He popped a cheese cube into his mouth. "Hey, Mom," he said.

"Hey, yourself," said Mom. She handed Traci a cheese cube. Traci chewed with her mouth open. Gooey cheese dribbled out of her mouth. Mom wiped Traci's chin.

"How was the first day of school?" She hugged Gus.

"Great, Mom," said Gus. He told her about Mr. D. About his earring. His ponytail. His parakeets.

"Can I get a dog?" Gus finished. "Brett's dog is going to have puppies."

"Gus, you know we can't," said Mom. "The apartment rules say no pets. And with the baby coming . . ." Mom patted her big round tummy.

Gus felt a twinge down in his tummy. He missed Oscar so much it hurt.

Mom put her arm around him and pulled him close. He burrowed his head under her arm. She smelled like talcum powder and graham crackers.

"Someday we'll have our own house," said Mom softly. "With a room of your own and a big backyard."

"Room for a dog?" asked Gus.

Mom laughed gently. "You don't give up, do you? Maybe. Maybe room for a dog," she said.

Traci banged her spoon on her high chair. Gus jumped.

"Oh, yeah!" he said. "I almost forgot!" He told Mom about the swimming pizza party.

"Can I go?" Gus practically panted with excitement.

"Sure," said Mom.

Gus slapped his hand to his forehead. The permission slip! The backpack!

Mom shook her head when he told her. Her blonde hair swung across her cheeks.

"What am I going to do with you, Gus?" she asked. "Listen to me. This is a new year. A new school. A new home. A fresh start. Last year . . . Well, you know how last year was. You couldn't seem to finish anything. You've got to pay attention, Gus. It's important."

"Sure, Mom," said Gus, cramming the last of the cheese cubes in his mouth. "I gotta go. I have to find my backpack."

"Be home soon," said Mom. "And don't slam the door."

"Right!" yelled Gus, slamming the door.

4. The Banshee

Gus left for school early the next morning. His backpack bounced on his back. Mom had signed the permission slip last night. Swimming party, here I come!

"RRRRooooowwwwwrrrrr!" Gus stopped short, skidding on the pavement like a baseball player sliding into home. What was that?

"RRRRooooowwwwwrrrrr!" It came again, louder this time. Gus peered around, uncertain. It sounded like a tiger. Or a siren. Or a banshee.

Gus knew what a banshee was. A wailing ghost who tried to grab you. He'd seen one in a horror movie. Goose bumps crawled across his flesh.

Footsteps came up behind him. The banshee! But it was only Pamela, clutching her backpack.

"What's that horrid noise?" she asked. "It sounds like a wet cat."

It did sound like a cat.

"Here, kitty, kitty," Gus called.

Small houses lined both sides of the street. Windows were shut, shades pulled. Garages were closed up tight. No kids were out. Just Gus and Pamela.

A slender, wimpy tree grew in a brown front yard. Gus looked up. He spied orange stripes.

"Hey!" said Gus. "It *is* a cat!"

Gus flung his backpack on the ground. "I'm going to get him."

"I read a book once where they called the fire department to rescue a cat."

"That was in the olden days," said Gus. "They don't do that anymore." Gus spit on his palms for traction and shimmied up the trunk. Lucky for him, there were a lot of trees in his old town.

He threw his leg over a branch. The cat was just above him, still yowling.

Gus reached out his hand. His voice was gentle. "Here, kitty," he called. "I won't hurt you."

The cat looked at him and hissed. His fur stuck up all over. His tail bristled.

Gus grabbed him around the tummy. He pulled. But the cat did not come down.

"What's happening?" yelled Pamela. "I can't see. Did you get him?"

Gus looked down into her upturned face. "No, he's stuck on something. I can't see what. Just a minute. I've got it."

The cat was caught on a piece of string around his neck. Gus's fingers felt it around the cat's neck. Some idiot had tied a string around the cat's neck. The string was caught on a tree branch. The more the cat struggled, the tighter it pulled. The string was like a noose, slowly strangling him. No wonder he yowled.

Gus pulled on the string, but it would not come loose.

Then a horrible thought struck him. He felt like he'd been punched in the gut. It was *his* string. *He* was the idiot who had tied the string around his neck! Thanks to him, this cat had nearly died.

"I can't get it. The string's too tight."

"You have to get it off, Gus Zander! Or that cat will starve to death or die of no water or strangle or something." She tapped her foot impatiently.

"The string is too tight," yelled Gus. "Do you have anything to cut it with? A pocket knife or something."

"Knives are not allowed at school," said Pamela in her goody-two-shoes voice. "But I think I have some scissors."

She unzipped her pencil case. "I've got some scissors. I'm coming up." Pamela put the scissors in her pocket. She shimmied up the trunk.

"How'd you do that?" asked Gus, taking the scissors. "I didn't know girls could climb trees."

Pamela gave him a withering look. "Idiot. Of course I can climb trees. I even have a tree fort. Which smart-alecky boys like you are not invited to." Pamela dropped to the ground.

"So, who's asking?" grumbled Gus. But he didn't waste much time replying. He had to save this cat.

He slid his fingers between the cat's neck and the string. He snipped the string. The cat was free.

The cat stopped yowling and went sort of limp. Gus scooped him up and dropped to the ground.

Pamela eyed him. "He's pretty ugly. If you ask me, he's a stray."

"I'm keeping this guy," said Gus. "I owe it to him. It's my fault he nearly died."

"If it was me, I'd turn him in to the pound," said Pamela. "He's really ugly."

"Never!" yelled Gus. His respect for her vanished. She was just what she seemed like at first, a bossy girl. He slung his backpack over his shoulders, the cat in his arms, and headed down the street.

"Well, all right for you, Gus Zander," called Pamela. "Just don't forget who had the scissors!"

5. A Cat Named Leo

The moment Gus got to school, he knew he'd have to hide the cat.

The bell had rung. The hallway was empty. Gus walked past Room 3, looking for a place.

There was a closed door at the end of the hall. Gus tried the knob. The door opened. Gus went in.

He was inside a small office. The lights were off. He had just time to make out a big comfy chair, a small window and a desk. A key hung on a chain by the door.

"What are you doing in Mr. Ryan's office?"

Gus jumped. Pamela had come in so quietly, he hadn't heard her. Gus slid the cat behind his back. The cat gave a little meow, then was quiet.

"Who's Mr. Ryan?"

"He's the counselor. He won't be here for two weeks because his wife had a baby. Weren't you listening when Mr. D told us?"

Pamela put her hands on her hips. "You'd better come out of here. Kids aren't supposed to be in here if Mr. Ryan isn't here. It's a school rule." She tapped her toe on the floor, like some old nosy busybody.

"You're not the boss of me," said Gus.

"I'm just telling you for your own good," she said and flounced off.

After Pamela left, Gus looked around. The office was warm. It was quiet. It was close to Gus's classroom. And best of all, it would be empty for two weeks.

In short, it was perfect. There was even a soft, comfy chair to sleep on!

Gus set the cat down. The cat licked his white paw and scrubbed his ear with it. Gus watched, pleased.

"A name," said Gus. "You need a name. Tiger? Too plain. Orangey? Too cutesy. You need a strong name. You need a name that makes you mine." The cat finished washing his ear and groomed his whiskers.

"I know!" said Gus. "I'll call you Leo. Leo means lion. It is a king's name, too."

He picked up a pencil and brushed the cat's head with it lightly. Interested, the cat stopped washing and batted the pencil. "I dub thee Sir Leo," said Gus. Leo looked pleased.

He hopped up on the chair and yawned, showing Gus his broken front tooth and pink tongue.

Gus yawned, too.

Finally, Leo walked around on the seat of the chair, making two complete circles, and settled down. He put his head under his paws, curled his tail over his nose, and went to sleep.

Of course. He'd had a long morning.

"I'll bring you some food at lunchtime," whispered Gus. "Something to drink, too."

Just before he left, Gus lifted the key off the hook by the door. He carefully locked the door behind him. Then he slipped the key into his pocket.

6. A Terrible, Horrible Menace

Gus planned to visit Leo at recess. But it didn't work out that way.

He didn't finish his math, so Mr. D told him to stay in. All the other kids went out to play. Gus glumly opened his book. He'd have to wait until lunch to see Leo.

Pamela stood by the bookshelf.

"Didn't you get the problems done, either?" Gus asked, surprised. Pamela looked like the kind of girl who always got her work done on time. He knew that kind of girl. Smart. Bossy.

"Of course I got my work done," snapped Pamela. "I'm staying in to help Mr. D sort reading books."

"Kids, can you manage?" said Mr. D. "I need to run to the office."

"Sure, Mr. D," said Pamela. Mr. D left.

Gus looked at his paper. He had only three problems left. Plenty of time. He bit the end of his eraser and tapped his hand against the seat of his chair.

Tweet-tweet. The parakeets. He'd almost forgotten about them. He got up to look at them more closely. Plenty of time to finish his math. Recess was fifteen minutes long. Three problems left. Five minutes per problem. No sweat.

He watched the parakeets.

There were two. A green one with yellow wings and black marks like freckles. And a blue one, the color of tropical seas. Mr. D had said the blue one was Peepers and the green one was Jeepers.

"Pish-pish." Gus made squeaking noises. The birds looked at him with shiny eyes. "Jeepers! Peepers!" He held his finger out.

"Ouch!" The green parakeet bit him. Gus put his finger in his mouth and sucked.

"You'd better get busy," said Pamela. She stopped sorting books. "Mr. D. will be back soon."

I don't think those birds get enough exercise," said Gus. "Living in a cage isn't the best. These are jungle birds. They need to fly around. I saw it on TV."

Pamela came over. "They look all right to me." She tossed her head.

"No, when they're cooped up, they get sick. Most people let them out for a while." Gus reached for the cage.

"I don't think you should do that."

Gus undid the latch and opened the door. "It's okay," he whispered. "Just a little recess time. For the birds. They need it, too."

But the parakeets didn't seem to want to come out. Gus reached into the cage, slowly, gently. He didn't want to scare them.

Pamela stood next to him. "The feathers look soft. Can I touch them, too?" she whispered.

"Sure," said Gus. "They'll sit on my finger. I'll bring one out."

The birds fluttered away from his hand. Jeepers flew to the top of the cage, but Peepers flew out the open door, brushing past Gus's hand and into the classroom.

"Now look what you've done!" shouted Pamela. "Mr. D will kill us!"

Gus turned around, and Jeepers shot out of the cage, too.

"Now they're both out! What are we going to do?" Pamela said.

The classroom seemed filled with birds. Could there be only two? Jeepers and Peepers darted from one end of the room to the other. Swooping low enough to brush the top of Gus's hair. Circling the ceiling lights.

"I guess they'll get enough exercise now," said Gus.

"Quick," said Pamela. "Close the door before they fly into the hall. We've got to get them back into their cage."

Gus hurried to shut the door. When he turned around, Pamela stood on top of Mr. D's desk.

"Here, birdie," she coaxed. Jeepers perched on the light above her head. Pamela stood on her tiptoes. She couldn't reach.

"You're taller," she said. "You do it."

Gus climbed up next to her. "Here, Jeepers," he called. He held out his finger, the way the man on TV had done.

Jeepers cocked his head. He inched closer. "Come on, birdie," whispered Gus. "You can do it."

Pamela took a deep breath.

Jeepers crept close to Gus's finger. BRRRRINGG! The recess bell rang.

Jeepers fluttered away in alarm.

The door opened. The class came in.

"Gosh, you guys!" said Brett. "What are you doing on Mr. D's desk?"

All the way down the hall, Pamela scolded Gus. "It's all your fault, Gus Zander!" she said. Her eyes were hot and angry. "I've never been sent to the principal in my whole life! My grandmother is going to be soooo mad! I wish you'd never moved here, Gus. You are nothing but trouble!"

"It wasn't my fault," said Gus. "How'd I know those birds would get away like that? Lucky for us they came when Mr. D whistled." Gus grinned when he remembered the bird poop on Pamela's desk.

But Pamela wasn't smiling. She shook her head so hard her red bow swayed.

"You are a menace, Gus Zander," she said. "A terrible, horrible menace."

Ms. Alvarez wasn't so bad, as principals went. She didn't yell or anything. She gave Gus a note to give to his parents when he got home.

At least he didn't get banned from the swimming party!

Oh, yeah! Gus slapped his forehead. The permission slip! He mustn't forget to turn it in. He'd do that as soon as he got back to class.

In fact, there was only one problem. Gus had to stay in the office every recess for the rest of the day. When could he visit Leo?

7. Pancakes and Elephant Jokes

Gus didn't see Leo until after school.

He hovered inside Mr. D's room, waiting until the kids were all gone.

"Where's your permission slip, Gus?" asked Mr. D.

Gus slapped his forehead. The swimming party! Mom was right. He really did need to pay attention. He burrowed in his backpack. The crumpled slip was not there. Gus searched frantically, unzipping all the compartments. At last he turned the bag upside down. No permission slip.

He shot an anguished look at Mr. D.

"I can't go?"

Mr. D smiled down at Gus. "We'll have to

work on your organizational skills this year," he said. "I'll give you another one. Bring it in tomorrow. But don't forget! You need that permission slip."

Gus stashed the new permission slip in his backpack. He tiptoed into the hall. The coast was clear. He unlocked the door to Mr. Ryan's office.

Gus slipped inside the office. He held the door carefully so Leo couldn't get out. He filled a bowl from the cafeteria with water from Mr. Ryan's sink. Leo drank. Gus sat back to watch.

Slowly, a smell tickled his nose. A bad smell. No. A stench! A horrid stink!

Under the counselor's big chair was a pile of cat poop.

Of course! Why hadn't he realized! A cat's gotta do what a cat's gotta do. Only one problem. What was he, Gus, going to do about it?

Well, he'd have to think about that later. He held his nose and pulled half a sandwich out of his backpack. "Hope you like peanut butter, Leo," he said.

Leo must have, or maybe he was just hungry, because he ate the whole thing. Gus stroked him.

It seemed to Gus that Leo looked better already. His torn ear had scabbed over. His eyes looked brighter. Gus was thrilled. His care was working after only one day. Just think what Leo would look like in a week! In a month!

"Got to go, Leo," he said regretfully. "I'll bring you more food tomorrow." And something to clean up the poop.

Bang! Bang! Bang! The sound of Traci banging on the crib woke Gus up. A thin gray light filtered through the shade. Good old Sis! She was better than any alarm clock.

"You want out, Sis?" he asked. He lifted her up and carried her into the kitchen.

"Pancakes, Gus?" asked Dad. He stood at the stove, holding a spatula. His face was stubbly. He hadn't shaved yet.

"Sure," said Gus. The floor was cold on his bare feet. He went to get dressed.

When he came back to the kitchen, Traci sat in her high chair. Dad cut a piece of pancake. Traci grabbed it with her fingers.

A plate full of golden brown pancakes sat on the table. "Help yourself," said Dad.

Gus stabbed a couple of cakes with his fork. He lifted them over to his plate. He spread butter on them and watched it melt into a golden pool. Then he drizzled syrup across the top.

"How come we're having pancakes today?" he asked. "It's not Saturday."

"I thought I'd make breakfast this morning," said Dad. "We'll let your mom sleep in. The baby kept her awake last night."

"How can it do that when it isn't even born yet?" asked Gus. He took a bite and chewed.

"It kicks in the night. Getting ready to be born, I guess."

"Ouch. That must hurt." Gus speared another bite.

"No," said Dad. "It doesn't hurt." He wiped Traci's face with a napkin and set her down on the floor.

"I've got a new joke," Dad said. "What's the difference between an elephant and a grape?"

Gus thought. "I don't know."

"Grapes are purple," said Dad.

Gus laughed so hard milk went up his nose. That made Traci laugh, too. After Gus cleaned himself up, Dad said, "You better hurry, Gus. Don't want to be late on the third day of school."

"Okay, Dad. Can you make my lunch?"

"Sure. Go get your backpack."

When Gus came out with his sweatshirt and backpack, he saw Traci toddling around. She couldn't walk very well yet. Her baby feet were fat and her knees had dimples. She chewed the ear of her favorite stuffed animal, a little golden lion.

A lion! Leo the lion! With a rush, Gus remembered Leo the cat. He grabbed the sack lunch Dad handed him, kissed him good-bye, and clattered down the stairs to the street. Up ahead, he saw Pamela's red bow swing on her ponytail.

He hoped Leo liked pickle sandwiches.

Gus visited Leo in Mr. Ryan's office every recess. He kept forgetting to bring something to put the poop in. And the pile under Mr. Ryan's chair grew bigger and smellier.

Leo wouldn't eat. He turned up his nose at pickle sandwiches. He ate turkey or peanut butter, but he wouldn't eat bananas at all. And he was restless.

Thursday, Gus arrived at school to find a crowd of kids around Mr. Ryan's door. His heart leaped into his mouth. Leo! They'd found Leo!

"Don't go near there," whispered Brett.

"Why not?" asked Gus. He had to get the kids away before they found Leo.

"It's haunted!" Brett's eyes were wide.

"Haunted?" Pamela shook her head and the red bow swung. "That's dumb. Ghosts aren't real."

"Well, that's what the fourth graders say," said Melanie. "Hannah heard weird noises coming from inside. Like this." She yowled.

Gus gulped. He knew that noise. Leo didn't like being locked up.

"And what about the awful smell?" added Zack. "How else can you explain that?"

Gus flinched. He kept forgetting to bring something to clean up the cat poop with.

Just then, Mr. D came out. "Time to come in, kids," he said. "We have to figure out how many pizzas we need if each pizza has eight slices and each child eats two."

When all the kids had gone back to class, Gus breathed a sigh of relief. Saved by math!

8. Caught!

On Friday, Gus gave Leo his sandwich. Leo sniffed. Maybe he didn't like tomatoes.

Gus didn't feel like eating, either. His stomach hurt. He still had to bring his permission slip. He had to figure out how to feed Leo over the weekend.

And he needed to deal with the cat poop.

He wanted to rescue Leo. But Leo acted like he was in prison, yowling and throwing himself at the door. Trying to get out.

If only there were someone he could tell! Mr. D? What would he say if he found out Gus had taken Mr. Ryan's key? Maybe he would ban Gus from the swimming party!

Mom or Dad? But they were counting on him to shape up this year. Pay attention. Think before acting. How could he tell them?

Gus leaned his chin on his hands. He felt hopeless.

Just then, the door crashed open. "What are you doing in here!" Pamela stood in the doorway. He'd forgotten to lock the door!

"Shhh!" hissed Gus. "Close the door! He'll get out!" He pulled Pamela into the office and shut the door.

"Who?"

"Shhh!" Gus tapped his fingers to his lips. "Remember that stray cat we found?"

"You've got a cat in here?" Pamela's voice rose. "I'm telling."

Gus shook his head. "Don't tell! He was homeless. He was hungry. He could have starved!"

"I don't care," said Pamela. "You're breaking the rules." She turned to go.

She saw the cat poop. "He did this? Yuck!"

"It's not his fault. A cat's gotta go sometimes," said Gus.

Pamela reached for the doorknob. If she leaves, I'm in hot water, thought Gus.

Just then, Leo headed straight for Pamela. He arched his back and rubbed up against her.

Pamela held stock-still, a cardboard cutout. She couldn't be scared, could she? Of a little bitty cat?

"It's okay," said Gus, gently. Whether to Leo or Pamela, he wasn't sure. He knelt down and scratched Leo's back. "He's friendly."

Pamela looked wary. "Go ahead," urged Gus. "He likes to be petted."

Pamela sat down slowly. "He won't bite?"

"No. I've tamed him." Gus petted Leo. Leo arched his back.

Pamela timidly put out her hand and touched Leo's fur. "He's soft," she said. She petted more strongly now.

"He looked so wild before," she said. "My grandmother won't let me have a pet. She says pets are dirty. She says they are a waste of money." She looked sad.

"Why do you live with your grandmother? Where's your mom and dad?"

Pamela stood up. She tossed her ponytail. "I don't have to tell you anything." She started toward the door.

"Don't go!" Gus called. "Wait. Forget it. Forget I asked. You don't have to tell me." He looked around desperately for something to keep her there.

Leo arched his back. "Look, Leo wants his back rubbed."

Pamela looked at Leo. She knelt back down and petted him again. Leo purred like a bumblebee. Pamela smiled.

"Okay. I guess I can tell you. My mom left when I was little. Sometimes I get a postcard from her. I lived with my dad until last year. He got a job on a fishing boat. He said he couldn't have me because he wouldn't be home much. My grandmother was the only one left."

"Gosh," said Gus. "That's bad."

"It's okay," said Pamela. "I love my grandmother."

But Gus noticed her mouth was sad. Maybe she wasn't bossy because she wanted to be. Maybe she was lonesome, too.

Pamela stroked Leo from head to tail. Leo rolled over on his back. "What's he doing?" asked Pamela in alarm.

"He just wants a belly rub," said Gus. He

scratched Leo under the chin and rubbed his white tummy.

Pamela scratched him. "What's his name?" she asked.

"Leo," said Gus.

Leo purred. He lifted his chin so the white bib showed.

"You won't tell, will you?" Gus asked. "He needs us."

Pamela's hand froze, mid stroke. "But we aren't supposed to be here. We'll get into trouble."

"Nobody will know."

"But it stinks. Someone will smell it."

Gus sighed. "I don't know what to do. I can't keep him. And you can't keep him. Stupid no pets rule. We can't let him go to the animal shelter!"

"We could make a litter box," said Pamela slowly.

"But how can we make a litter box? And cat food? He won't eat sandwiches." He felt close to tears. He must save Leo. But there were so many problems!

Pamela stood up. She brushed off her clothes, all business again. "Leave it to me."

"You! You don't know anything about cats!"

"Maybe not, but I know how to use the library. And I know how to do research. And I know how to make things. And," she said fiercely, "I have seven dollars. Plenty of money to buy cat food."

Gus looked up at her. She took a long time to make up her mind, but when she did, she was sure bossy. But it was a good kind of bossy. Probably just what he and Leo needed. A plan. Some organization. A partner.

"You're on," he said.

"Step one," said Pamela. "Meet me here after school. We'll make a litter box and get some cat food."

Good. Now, if only he could get his permission slip signed!

9. Pamela in Charge

With Pamela in charge, Gus figured his problems were over.

He was wrong.

They met outside the apartment building after school. "Bring dirt," said Pamela. "We absolutely have to make a litter box."

"What about food?" asked Gus.

Pamela wrinkled her nose. "First things first."

Pamela had brought a plastic dishpan from her house. Gus filled it with dirt.

Gus carried it back to the school. Pamela carried a bag of dry cat food and six plastic bowls. She'd bought the cat food with her own money. The bowls were from her apartment.

"How will we get in?" asked Gus.

Pamela smiled. "No problem. There's basketball practice this afternoon. The school will be open."

They slipped into Mr. Ryan's office and set down the litter box and the bag of food. They cleaned up the mess. Gus wanted to play with Leo, but Pamela was strict.

"We don't have much time," she said. "We have to be home by dinner. Let's leave enough food for the weekend." She petted Leo and went to work.

Gus filled three bowls with water. Pamela poured food into the others.

"Good-bye Leo," said Gus. He scratched Leo behind the ears. "See you Monday."

They met in Pamela's tree fort on Saturday.

"Wow," said Gus when he saw it.

"I built it myself," said Pamela proudly.

The fort was in a vacant lot next to the apartment building. Pamela had nailed a few boards to some branches. An orange crate nailed to one limb made a shelf.

I could make this into something good, thought Gus, looking around. If she'd let me help.

They ate pretzels and planned out their strategy. Pamela had brought the pretzels. "They're healthy for you," she said. "They have no fat."

Gus didn't care. He ate them anyway.

Pamela also brought a chart, drawn in colored pencils. It showed days and times, who would feed Leo and when. It made Gus dizzy just to look at it. Sheez, he thought, what did I get myself into now?

On Monday, Gus and Pamela walked to school together. Pamela gave Leo a catnip mouse.

Gus felt a little jealous so he pulled Pamela's hair bow off.

"Stop that!" yelled Pamela. "You want my help or don't you?"

Gus stopped. But he still felt jealous. I hope Leo won't like her better than me, thought Gus.

Pamela was like a general. A bossy old general. And I'm the little green army man, Gus thought.

Still, things were better. There was no longer a pile of cat poop under Mr. Ryan's chair. Pamela made him empty the cat box every day, so the office didn't stink anymore.

Everyday at recess, Gus and Pamela slipped into Mr. Ryan's office. Gus invented games to play with Leo. He'd put his coat over Leo and say "Where's the cat?" Leo would pounce on his fingers. Leo loved that.

Gus didn't miss Oscar so much anymore. Now he had Leo.

Now that Gus and Pamela visited, Leo didn't yowl to be let out. Kids stopped saying the office was haunted.

The cat food was good for him. Gus couldn't see Leo's ribs anymore. And his fur was softer, more like a pet-store kitty. Gus could put up with anything, even Pamela, if Leo was happy.

On Thursday, Pamela even organized Gus's permission slip. "Don't forget it, Gus," she told him. "Bring it tomorrow. Or no pizza for you."

She made a big note in pencil. PERMISSION SLIP!!!! DON'T FORGET!!! She pinned it to his backpack. It looked dorky, like a kindergarten baby. Gus could put up with it. Anything not to miss the swimming party!

"My dad's picking me up tonight," Pamela reminded him. "He's taking me to the beach for the whole weekend. You'll have to feed Leo and leave enough food and water. I'll miss the party."

"I wish you could come," he told her.

She looked at him. "You do?"

"Sure. We could have a water fight. We could have a pizza eating contest."

Pamela rolled her eyes. She tossed her ponytail. "Just don't forget to hand in your permission slip tomorrow," she told him. "Or you'll miss the party, too."

Just before Gus left for school Friday morning, Mom said, "Don't forget. I'm picking you up right after school. Traci has a checkup today."

"No sweat, Mom," yelled Gus as he ran out the door.

"And don't slam the door," said Mom.

"Right," yelled Gus, slamming the door.

Pamela wasn't in school. Gus almost forgot to hand in his permission slip. But he saw the note when he hung up his backpack.

"Swimming party, here I come!" he yelled. He gave the note to Mr. D.

"Just in time!" said Mr. D. "I thought you weren't going to make it!" He laughed. "Glad to see you're working on those organizational skills!"

Gus laughed, too. But silently he thanked Pamela.

The class worked hard all day. They wrote stories in their journals about swimming pools and pizzas. They solved fraction problems with cardboard pizzas. They estimated how many gallons of water it would take to fill a swimming pool.

At recess, Gus visited Leo. He cleaned his cat box and filled his bowls with food and water. Leo looked around. "She'll be back on Monday," Gus told him.

At the end of the day, Mr. D gave out a list. "Don't forget," he said. "Swim suit! Money for snacks! Towel!"

Gus crammed the list into his backpack. No way he'd forget!

As the class lined up to go home, Ms. Alvarez's voice came over the intercom.

"Just a reminder," said Ms. Alvarez. "The school will be fumigated on Saturday to get rid of pests. The treatment might make animals sick, so all classroom pets should be taken home."

"What does fumigate mean?" asked Brett.

"Bug spray," said Mr. D. "They're going to

spray pesticide around the school to kill termites, fleas, carpenter ants. Pests like that."

"Ick," said Melanie. She held her nose.

"Well, obviously it wouldn't be good for people. That's why they're doing it on Saturday. And it wouldn't be good for pets, either. Maybe after the fumigation, we'll get another pet," added Mr. D. "In the meantime, I'll take Jeepers and Peepers home tonight. We wouldn't want those little guys to get sick!"

Mr. D winked. "And because of the fumigators, the bus for the swimming party will pick us up at the city park. The bus will leave at nine o'clock, sharp. Don't be late. We can't wait for stragglers."

Gus's heart leapt into his mouth. What about Leo! He wouldn't be safe at school with the bug spray! What should he do?

He couldn't take Leo now. Mom would pick him up in a few minutes. Gus wished Pamela was here. She'd know what to do. But Pamela was at the beach with her dad.

What would Pamela do? Gus chewed his pencil. She'd come back after school and rescue Leo. The building would be open for basketball practice. But what if he forgot? Pamela wouldn't forget. Gus chewed his lip. Then he took a red marker and printed a note: RESCUE LEO.

Gus pinned his note to his backpack with the safety pin. It looked dorky, but it would remind him. Jeeze, he thought. I'm even starting to think like her.

"Hey, Gus," said Mom. She stood in the classroom doorway. Traci sat on her hip. She giggled when she saw Gus.

"Ready to go, big guy?"

Gus nodded and grabbed his backpack.

As they drove out of the parking lot, Gus saw Mr. D putting the birdcage into his car.

Don't forget to rescue Leo, he told himself. It's important.

10. "Rescue Leo!"

Gus sat in the doctor's waiting room. Mom took Traci in for her checkup.

He swung his legs against his backpack. The office lady glared. "Read a magazine," she said.

Gus looked at the magazines on the table. They looked boring. He held his backpack by the strap and spun it around so it twisted up. He watched it untwist, faster and faster. The red letters on the note spun around.

RESCUE LEO! RESCUE LEO! RESCUE LEO!

That was fun so he did it again. Twist, twist, twist. Spin, spin, spin. It made him kind of dizzy to watch.

He liked the noise it made. *Brrrupt! Brrrupt! Brrrupt!* He did it again.

It must have made the office lady dizzy, too. Or maybe she didn't like the noise. Because she came out from behind her desk and grabbed his backpack.

"I'll just keep this for you until you leave," she said.

Gosh. She sounded like a teacher.

After that, there wasn't anything to do but wait.

Mom came out of the examining room. "Time to go, Gus," said Mom. She held Traci on her hip. Traci grinned. She held a pink balloon.

Gus leaped up and followed them out the door. He couldn't wait to get home. He had to get ready for the swimming party tomorrow!

"It's hot in here," said Mom when they got home. "How about a barbecue?"

Gus carried silverware and plates, lemonade, hot dogs and buns downstairs to the little apartment play yard.

The warm fall evening was perfect for a picnic. The sun made long shadows across the playground.

Gus and his family sat at a picnic table. Dad grilled hot dogs on the portable barbecue. Traci rocked in the baby swing.

"Want another hot dog?" called Dad. He waved the tongs.

"Sure," said Gus. He picked up a bun and held it open. Dad slid the hot dog into the bun.

"I've got another joke for you," said Dad. "How did the elephant hide in the cherry tree?"

Gus poured mustard on his hot dog and took a bite. "I don't know. How?"

"He painted his toenails red!" said Dad with a big grin.

Gus laughed.

"Time for bath and then bed," said Mom, all too soon.

"No," said Gus. Something nagged him. Something he had to do?

"You have to get up early tomorrow, Gus. The bus leaves from the city park at nine o'clock sharp!"

That was it! Gus jumped up. "My swimming trunks!" he yelled. "My towel! My wallet!"

Gus rushed around. He gathered up his trunks and a towel. He couldn't find his backpack, so he shoved them in a purple sports bag. He found his wallet under his bed. It was empty. Oh, yeah. He'd spent all his money on candy.

"Can I have some money for snacks, Dad?" he begged.

Dad clicked his tongue. "You'll have to learn to manage better than that, Gus," he said. "Money doesn't grow on trees, you know. Not like cherries!"

"Or elephants!" said Gus.

Dad laughed and gave Gus two dollars.

Finally Gus was ready for bed. Mom tucked him in. Just before he fell asleep, a stray thought drifted through his mind. Was there something he'd forgotten?

Moonlight streamed into Mr. Ryan's office. Leo wasn't asleep. His eyes gleamed. He sat on the windowsill, his paws curled underneath him, looking outside. He was as still as a little sphinx. And just as peaceful.

II. Buzz Off!

Gus overslept. He didn't hear Traci banging on her crib until it was too late for breakfast. He jumped into yesterday's school clothes. No time to be picky. He grabbed the bag with his towel and trunks. He stuffed his wallet into his pocket.

"Bye, Mom!" he yelled. "Bye, Dad! Bye, Traci!"

Mom kissed him, and handed him a granola bar. "Have fun!"

He ran down the stairs and past the apartment building. The street was just ahead.

The big yellow school bus rumbled past. On its way to the city park! He'd have to run. Swimming party! Pizza party! I'm coming! Don't go without me!

But just as he started to run, a van drove past, heading the other way. Heading toward the school.

It was white, with red and black letters: BUZZ OFF PEST REMOVAL.

On top sat a huge cockroach. The wings and legs vibrated in the wind.

Gus stopped in his tracks. Buzz Off! Pest Removal? The fumigators! Today! At school! Leo!

His heart pounded against his chest so hard it hurt. He'd forgotten all about Leo. Leo locked in the building, helpless, and the pest control people on the way!

Down at the opposite corner, the bus headed toward the city park. If he went back for Leo, he'd miss the swimming party.

Gus's feet were rooted to the spot. The party: the pizza, the water fights, the snacks. Or Leo?

All at once, his feet unlocked from the pavement. Move, he cried to his legs! His legs moved. He pounded down the street, arms and legs pumping, his breath tearing his lungs.

The pest control van parked in the school parking lot. Three men in orange jumpsuits

were hooking up huge white hoses. They wore gas masks. Gus didn't stop. He rounded the corner and dashed up the front stairs.

"Hey! Kid! You can't go in there!" shouted one man.

Gus tore down the empty hallway to Mr. Ryan's office. He turned the key. Leo tumbled out, into his arms.

12. Gus to the Rescue

The pest control men crowded around. Gus held Leo tight.

"I had to save him!" he panted. His breath came in ragged spurts. Leo squirmed.

"Okay, kid," said a pest control man. His eyes were kind above his mask, "You got him. Now you've got to get out. We have work to do."

Gus cuddled Leo to his chest. He walked out of the building, down the stairs. The sports bag bumped against his knees. Leo meowed in protest. If only he had a cat carrier! But they were too much money.

He did have a carrier! He unzipped his bag and set Leo on top of his towel. He closed the bag partway. Leo's head poked out. Leo seemed to like it.

Gus took Leo to Pamela's tree fort. He slung the bag over his shoulder and climbed up. Once there, he opened the bag. Leo stepped out. He looked around.

Gus scratched him under the chin.

"What am I going to do with you?" he said.

Just then, Pamela scrambled up.

"But I thought you were at the beach!" said Gus.

"We had to come back early," said Pamela. "My dad got called back to work." She saw Leo. "What's up?"

Gus told her all about his rescue.

"You chose Leo over the swimming party?" Pamela looked impressed. "I didn't know you had it in you!"

Pamela tickled Leo under his chin. "I guess we'll have to take him to the animal shelter after all."

Gus clenched his fists. "No way! There's got to be a better answer!"

"But what? You can't keep him. I can't keep him. We can't leave him in Mr. Ryan's office

anymore. The two weeks are up. Remember? Mr. Ryan will be back Monday."

Gus thought about the litter box and food bowls. He'd really left Mr. Ryan's office a mess.

"There isn't anything else to do," repeated Pamela.

"If we take him to the shelter and no one adopts him, he'll be put to sleep. I'm not letting that happen!" Gus grabbed Leo so tightly, Leo mewed.

Pamela put her hands on her hips. "Then just what do you think we can do?"

"We have to tell Mr. D," Gus said.

"No!" said Pamela. "He'll call our folks. He'll tell the principal. We'll get into trouble. My grandmother will be soooo mad!"

"We have to," insisted Gus. "I need to return the key I took. We need to clean Mr. Ryan's office. We need someplace to keep Leo. We have to tell. It's the right thing to do."

They argued, but in the end, Pamela saw that Gus was right. On Monday, Gus would bring Leo to school in the carrier bag, and they would tell.

Pamela sighed. "You are a horrible menace, Gus," she said softly. "A terrible, horrible menace. If I'd never met you, I'd never be in this trouble."

Gus looked at her. "But aren't you glad anyway?" He pointed to Leo. His orange fur was soft, his eyes bright.

Pamela stroked the cat. "Yes," she said. "It was worth it. Whatever happens."

13. Gus Makes a Plan

They kept the cat in Gus's dad's office Saturday and Sunday nights. Luckily, Dad didn't go in that weekend. On Monday morning, Gus and Pamela walked to school together. Gus carried the purple sports bag. Leo's head poked out the top. His pink nose twitched at all the smells.

Mr. D was surprised to meet Leo. Pamela told him the whole story, even about Gus's choosing to rescue Leo instead of going to the swimming party.

Mr. D scratched Leo behind the ears. "It sounds like you guys have your hearts in the right places," he said. "But what you've done is serious. I'll need to call your parents, Gus, and Pamela's grandmother."

Pamela sighed. Gus knew she was dreading it. He punched her lightly on the shoulder. "It's okay, Pamela," he said. "I'll be there, too."

Afternoon sun spilled into Ms. Alvarez's office, warming the room. Leo curled up in Gus's lap. Gus petted him. Stroking Leo calmed him.

Dad sat next to him. Behind the desk sat Ms. Alvarez. Her black hair was slicked back into a bun. Large hoop earrings wobbled as she wrote something down on a pad of paper.

Pamela came in with her grandmother. Gus had seen her at the apartment building, but never met her. She had fluffy brown hair. She wore running shoes and a fanny pack. They sat across from Gus.

Next, Mr. D came in. All the chairs were full, so he sat on the edge of the windowsill.

Gus shot him a worried glance. Was he angry? He winked. Gus felt better.

Pamela's face was white. No red bow in her hair today. She perched on her chair with her hands clasped in her lap. She didn't smile.

"What you did is serious," began Ms. Alvarez. Her gold hoops swayed. "You stole a key. You used a schoolroom without permission. You kept a stray cat on school grounds. It was unhealthy, unsafe, and unsanitary."

Gus's stomach did flip-flops. Pamela bit her lip.

"I can see that you meant well. But you made some bad choices."

Pamela's chin came up. "We're sorry, Ms. Alvarez," she said.

Dad nudged Gus.

"I'm sorry, too," Gus said.

"I appreciate that," said Ms. Alvarez, "but there needs to be action as well. First, you must return the key and apologize to Mr. Ryan. Second, you need to clean his office."

"We can do that," said Pamela. "But what about Leo? We can't send him to the shelter!"

Just then, Leo jumped to the floor. He yawned and stretched. A piece of lint caught his eye and he pounced. He tossed it into the air and lept up. It looked like he was dancing. Everyone laughed.

"Can't we keep him at school?" said Gus. "Mr. D could have him for a classroom pet. He said he wanted another one."

Mr. D laughed. "I meant a hamster or an iguana," he said. "Not a cat."

Leo stopped dancing and began to prowl. He went from person to person, sniffing everyone's shoes. When he got to Mr. D, he rubbed against his legs. Mr. D bent down. He scratched under Leo's chin.

Ms. Alvarez shook her head. "I'm afraid we can't have cats at school. It's too distracting. And many children are allergic to cats. Food and vet bills are expensive, as well."

Leo nodded as if he'd made up his mind. He jumped to the windowsill next to Mr. D and stepped into his lap.

"How about you, Mr. D?" asked Gus. "Leo likes you. You need a cat! To keep away the mice!"

Pamela joined in. "And cats are great friends. They are smart and funny. Since you live alone, Leo would be good company for you."

"And we could visit him!" said Gus.

Leo rubbed his head against Mr. D as if to say he agreed. His loud purr filled the room.

Mr. D laughed and held up his hands. "I can see I've been chosen," he said. "Very well, I'll adopt Leo."

"Thanks, Mr. D. That'd be great!" said Gus.

"Can we come visit?" asked Pamela.

Mr. D smiled. "No problem. I'd love to have you both. And Leo will love it, too."

Ms. Alvarez continued. "That's one matter taken care of. But I feel there needs to be something more."

She turned to Dad and Mrs. Kennedy. "What do you think?"

The grown-ups talked on, but Gus stopped listening. Leo was going home with Mr. D! No more scrambling for food. No more disease or cat fights. No more sleeping outside or escaping from dogs.

But how he'd miss that cat! Sure, he could visit, but he wouldn't see Leo every day. Gradually, he became aware that someone was talking to him.

"Do you understand?" asked Ms. Alvarez.

"Huh?" said Gus.

Mr. D looked up. "Gus, you and Pamela are going to need to do some community service."

Oh, no! That sounded awful.

"Three days a week, after school, we want you to volunteer at the animal shelter. Cleaning pens and feeding animals."

Wow! Animals almost every day! That was terrific. Gus looked at Pamela. She was smiling.

"Can you do that, Gus?" asked Mr. D.

Sure, he could do that.

After all, he had Pamela to help. He knew that kind of girl. Straight As. Bossy. And pretty cool.

How to Care for Stray Cats

Gus knew he'd made some mistakes when he tried to rescue Leo, so when Mr. D asked him to write a report about stray cats, he jumped at the chance. Here's Gus's report.

Stray Cats
by
Gus Zander

If you find a stray cat, do not put a string around its neck. Strings can catch on branches or trees and choke him. Get a grown-up to help you catch the cat. First leave out some food and call the cat. When the cat comes to eat, put it in a box or cat carrier.

If it is a mama cat, do not take it away. It might have kittens hidden nearby.

Second, find out if the cat is homeless or just lost. You can put up signs around the neighborhood telling people you found a cat. If no one answers, you can keep the cat.

Third, take the cat to the vet. The doctor will check the cat to see if it's healthy. Stray cats can be injured or sick. A vet can give your cat medicine. A vet can also give the cat a flea bath. And a vet can spay or neuter the cat. Spay the cat if it is a girl cat; neuter it if it is a boy cat. That's so they won't have kittens. This is very important because if your cat has kittens, the kittens might end up as stray cats, too.

Do not keep your cat at school unless the teacher says it is okay.

Your cat needs healthy food, not sandwiches. It needs fresh water every day. It needs a litter box. You have to dump the dirty litter every day, but it isn't too gross.

Cats are good pets. They are soft. They are funny. They purr when they are happy. Best of all, cats are good friends.